You must buy this brilliant bo
but like anything Milly Johnso
funny but also sometimes wa
heart
Dave & Si aka The

Fabulous, funny poems and benefitting cats, what more could you want? Milly has brilliant, hilarious insight into all our many neuroses and quirks.
Jane Fallon, novelist

Warm, witty and perceptive poems on behalf of those furry führers we foolishly consider to be our pets. Malcolm, our Burmese, knows full well that the boot is on the other paw.
Garry Bushell, columnist and author

It's hard to convey through mere words just how great cats are, but Milly has successfully done just that.
Larry the Cat, 10 Downing Street, London

A selection of funny and heart-warming poems with real CAT-itude. Be forewarned: you will laugh out loud!
Samantha Giles, actress

I've known Milly for years and have always admired her energy and 'sparkle' (never mind the talent), so I applaud her efforts to support 'Yorkshire Cat Rescue', it's typical of her that she's thrown herself into this project and no surprise to learn she's doing it for 'nowt'. I urge you to buy this book of poems, ALL proceeds are going to the charity.
Bernie Clifton, comedian, entertainer, broadcaster and ostrich jockey

Having known Milly's work and her tireless commitment to cats in their every form, this will be a delightful read especially if you are a devotee of the little devils. Also, the book will make a beautiful, all year gift. I hope you enjoy it.
Su Pollard, actress, singer, entertainer

Contents

Introduction

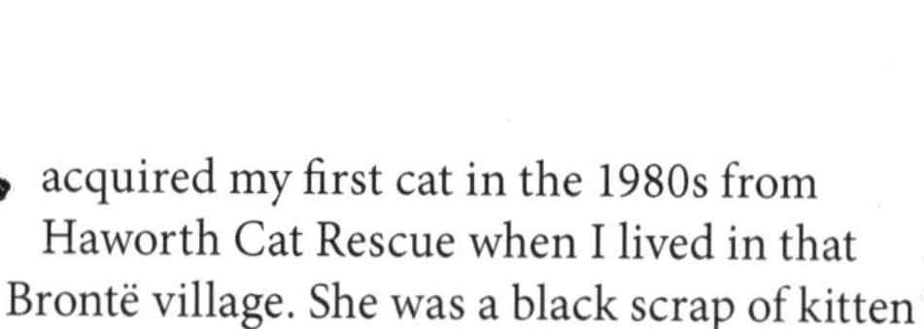

I acquired my first cat in the 1980s from Haworth Cat Rescue when I lived in that Brontë village. She was a black scrap of kitten that I adopted to keep my dog company when I was at work. I named her Guinness and she stole my heart. Since then I have never been without at least two cats in the house and I have loved them all – pedigrees and moggies, each with their own unique personality. That small rescue centre grew into Yorkshire Cat Rescue and I have become their patron.

It is a wonderful charity and I know that all the money it raises goes to where it should ie the cats and not on 'fat cat' wages and swanky office furniture. Trust me, I have seen their offices and it definitely doesn't go there.

I've been asked by a few people to publish the poems I've written and so here they are, with a few words about them so you can see which seed they sprouted from in my head (note: they are meant to be performed so scan better when spoken aloud). I thought, if I was going to sell them, it seemed a good idea to do it for charity, so all the profits will go to the rescue centre.

They are always on the look out for things to raffle off or QUALITY resellable items for their charity shops, blankets and towels and of course, monetary contributions and legacies without which they couldn't survive.

Plus they always need kind people who have a quiet home and a loving ***cat-shaped space*** on their lap waiting to be filled.

I hope you enjoy my poetry and Stu's most excellent illustrations. And thank you for buying this and contributing to such a worthy cause.

Yorkshire Cat Rescue
Lower Pierce Close
Cross Roads
Keighley
BD22 9AQ

Tel: 01535 647184
mail@yorkshirecatrescue.org

Web: https://yorkshirecatrescue.org
Twitter: @yorkscatrescue

The New Cat

Remember that your true vocation
Is to look at me with adoration
Pay my mortgage, be my host
My masseuse and my scratching post
Feed me salmon and prime cod
And foods that doth befit a god
Whilst in your joy I punch a hole
When I prefer a scabby vole
Open doors when I demand
My wishes should be your command
Fulfil my every want and need
The newspaper you spread to read
Is mine to sprawl on more than yours
I'll block the words with all four paws
Sometimes I may choose to spray
And watch you trying to scrub away
My lovely scent – it's all in vain
For I'll be spraying there again
Scoop my poop and clean my litter
Post my photographs on Twitter

And permit me please to verify
The dog is mine to terrify
I think it's fairly orthodox
That I would choose a cardboard box
Above your fluffy, furry dome
That cost a mint, from Pets at Home
Love me and you just might find
I stoop occasionally to be kind
I'll rub my cheek along your skin
And butt my head against your chin
A mere concession - don't forget
I am an idol, not a pet

I have no idea why we love cats as we do considering they rule the roost and disregard all rules. If my son was like that, I'll be having words. This poem is what I'd imagine a cat would say to his new owner, setting out his stall. How lucky you are to have HIM!

Graduands

My friends left our house today
Suddenly our four years of
    Laughter, fears
    Confessions, tears
Echoed like ghosts
    Through their hollow rooms
The silence shouts
No plants or posters anywhere
Just a bed with folded woollen sheet
    A table and a chair
A large window where the sunshine
    Bounces in and
                off the
                        Blu Tack traces on the walls

In the time between finishing your degree exams and graduating, you are officially a 'graduand'. I was twenty-two and university life was over. My two best pals left for home in the morning as I was leaving in the afternoon. The house felt so incredibly lonely, and I felt drenched with sadness that it was the end of an era. The bright sunny day was at odds with my mood and I walked around the house we shared and into their empty rooms. The sight of blobs of Blu Tack, which once fastened all their bright posters and happy photos to the walls, made me a bit weepy. I scribbled this down just before the taxi arrived.

Gin Goggles

You'll see him in a nightclub
He stands out from the crowd
That Mr Darcy lookalike
Handsome, tall and proud
You'll talk and flirt, he'll take you home
'A coffee?' you'll suggest
And then before you know it
He'll have jumped upon your chest
And in the morning sunlight
You'll turn with eyes adoring
But all you'll find's a big fat slob
Slavering, farting, snoring
So if you want to get a man
Who makes you melt and swoon
Stay away from G & Ts
And stick to Mills & Boon

The female equivalent of Beer Goggles: when people look so much more attractive at night after a few gins than they do in the morning when you wake up sober. Not written from personal experience obviously.

The Menopause

Sharon has started to sweat a lot
She's abandoned her nightie and slippers
She now goes to her bed
Dressed from feet up to head
In a wet suit with snorkel and flippers

With the cash she'd save not buying tampons
Mags was going to buy a Mercedes
But the brass in her banks
Has all gone on Spanx
Health supplements and TENA Ladies

Caroline's hobbling and wobbling
She needs two new hips and new knees
Her joints are as stiff
As a teddy boy's quiff
And she throws her back out with one sneeze

She used to walk tall in stilettos
In the old days she'd out-dance St Vitus
Now all she can handle
Is a Dr Scholl's sandal
Thanks to gout and plantar fasciitis

Jane was too vain to wear glasses
Her world was a dim blurry mess
She's now rather vocal
On the joys of bifocals
And owns more specs than Vision Express

Sam's been backpacking all over the world
New Zealand, the Congo, Madrid
But now what she'd choose
Is a nice Saga cruise
Or a 'Turkey and Tinsel' in Brid

Dawn used to down pints of snakebike in one
She was Yorkshire's own female George Best
But she's stopped getting drunk
Cos her bladder has shrunk
And she daren't risk her pants getting messed

Pam goes upstairs then says 'Why am I here?'
She thinks something is wrong with her head
'Where's my phone, where's my keys
Did I feed the Burmese?
What's the name of the bloke in my bed?'

Tracey's got hair springing out everywhere
It's turned her right into a stress head
She waxes, she lasers
She plucks, cuts and razors
And still she looks like Brian Blessed

Jude's moods are swinging all over the place
One minute she's crying and down
She's depressed about death
Then in the next breath
She's cackling like Coco the clown

Jan's spent so much money on hair dye
She could have bought Edinburgh Castle
She's now stopped her excesses
With the result that her tresses
Are the colour of Kris Kringle's arsehole

Sue's nickname at school was 'Pipe Cleaner'
But now she wears size thirty clothes
Last year when in Spain
Her bra snapped from the strain
And her tits dropped and broke all her toes

Karen's a chronic insomniac
She lies there and stares at the moon
But she's trying meditation
Sex, inebriation
And box sets of Terry and June

HRT has transformed Joanne's sex life
She stands on the rooftops to shout
That she's back in the sack
Her libido's come back
And she's no longer got a dry clout

Natalie's bowel has a mind of its own
Her farting is hard to ignore
With a silent but deadly
And a long trumpet medley
She once cleared a whole Morrisons store

But keep it all in some perspective
We're lucky to be here to age
There's still laughs a-plenty
In years long past twenty
There's fun to be had at each stage

Whilst we're moaning at deafness and grey hair
Whilst we're griping at middle-aged spread
Carpal tunnel, arthritis
High winds and cystitis
We're breathing, we're not bloody dead

After taking mental notes of all the MANY symptoms of the Menopause that pals of mine were going through, I thought I'd pen this. What a dreadful sea the Menopause is to navigate. If we didn't laugh at it, we would cry!

Apron Strings

My apron strings are pulling tight
It's just a case of time
Before the ties will snap outright
But the pain will all be mine

For it is a mother's curse
To learn that I will slide
From the centre of your universe
Out to the farthest side

Once you were my cargo
My breath was your breath too
Your lullaby - my heartbeat
I've have died, still would, for you

I won't forget the joy
Of that final bloody push
Of them saying 'it's a boy'
And love coming at a rush

The first smile that lit my heart up
Your first steps for mankind
I've pressed them all like flowers
In the pages of my mind

Story books, you on my lap
Whilst sucking on your thumb
When you first called me 'mummy'
When did it change to mum?

If only I had known it
I'd have savoured that last time
When your arms came out towards me
Or your little hand sought mine

Your radar's full of mates now
And phones and music mixes
Computer games with shooting and
Zombie apocalypses

I'm useful as a taxi
Who doesn't charge a fare
A presence in the background
Invisible as air

You hear nothing that I tell you
Though I play merry hell
I'm just bank of mum
And home's becomes hotel

My worry nerve is cranked to max
And every night I pray
You'll be sensible and happy
Safe, to see another day

The more love that I gave you
The more I set you free
The easier I made it for you to go
The harder I made it for me

We bring our chicks into the world
We give them all our best
The food, the time, the guidance
Protection of the mother nest

But chicks are meant to fly
And if our job is properly done
Their wings will have grown strong enough
To take them to the sun

Those apron strings will break
But you'll stay in my heart always
With Easter bunnies, birthday cake
And bonkers Christmas days

With cards made out of egg boxes
School pantomimes and plays
Wrapped up in memories as sweet
As Mother's Day bouquets

My two sons are grown up now and when my younger son went to university I was distraught. I've loved being a mother and his leaving home made me very reflective. I think it's the hardest part of being a mum when they strike out for independence and leave the safe harbour you offer them for uncharted waters – i.e. their own lives.

The Trollop of Scunthorpe

She set her thieving eyes upon
The first love that I doted on
Worse than the whore of Babylon
The Trollop of Scunthorpe

I was just a shy nineteen
She was a walking sex machine
She pounced, just like that tart Jolene
The Trollop of Scunthorpe

She worked with him, this flighty bird
In the Co-op, so I heard
He dropped me like a red hot turd
For the Trollop of Scunthorpe

Because she flirted and they chatted
Because his faithless butt was flattered
My poor heart was left broke and shattered
By the Trollop of Scunthorpe

She organised their wedding do
This cow who was my Waterloo
No thought to what she'd put me through
The Trollop of Scunthorpe

I sank into a deep abyss
Whilst my first love begot two kids
And lived a life of wedded bliss
With the Trollop of Scunthorpe

But what doesn't kill you makes you stronger
I decided I'd be sad no longer
This deep resentment I would conquer
Of the Trollop of Scunthorpe

I wiped my eyes and blew my nose
And like a phoenix up I rose
A tale I started to compose
About a Trollop from Scunthorpe

I wrote a book, it went to print
It sold a stack, I made a mint
It was about an evil bint
A Trollop from Scunthorpe

Twenty years and more went past
Still, any fool could have forecast
That houses built on shit don't last
Especially in Scunthorpe

On their silver anniversary
My first true love cut loose and free
And she became a divorcée
The Trollop from Scunthorpe

And me? I reap the dividend
I'm happy with a new boyfriend
I think no more of that bellend
And the Trollop of Scunthorpe

My first love dumped me very unceremoniously for a woman he met at work. I had a total emotional meltdown, but if he hadn't done it I wouldn't have gone off to spend my summer holidays in Wales and (long story) I wouldn't have encountered the wonderful actress Shirley Stelfox who gave me a proper talking-to and made me promise to give a writing career my best shot. Typically I blamed the Trollop of Scunthorpe in the beginning until age and experience eventually taught me that my ex was the bigger twat.

Barry and Cath

Everyone needs a beacon in life
To light up the way of their path
I had two of the greatest there were
In novelists – Barry and Cath

Whenever I doubted I'd do it
On those days when all my hopes fell through
Whenever I felt on the road to nowhere
I'd think of this wonderful two

I worried at forty I was too old to start
But I heard their wise words clear as day
'To each and all things there's a time, lass
Write when you've summat to say

Write from your heart as well as your brain
Use what we did as a guide
Write where you come from always with love
And write where you come from with pride

Let your voice reflect all the best bits of the north
Be true to your roots in each word
Let age, sex nor background impede you
And you'll fly like a Barry Hines bird'

These two are much more than the sums of their books
They've been with me each step on my path
As authors I read, and as teachers that led
There's none better than Barry and Cath

There are two literary giants who kept me hoping that one day I would make it as a novelist: Barry Hines and Catherine Cookson. Both writers who bucked the trend and wrote provincial stories that sold by the millions. Barry was a Barnsley lad and gave me a love of literature and, after reading his most iconic work 'A Kestrel for a Knave' he also instilled in me a passion for flying birds of prey which I do as often as I can at the Falconry Centre in Thirsk (www.falconrycentre.co.uk). Catherine was over forty when she had her first book published, but she still managed to sell over 123 million books to date. I really mean it when I say that on days when I thought 'I'll never be published' these two shining examples popped into my head and said, 'Well, we did it!' And so did I in the end.

The Great Big Pot of Tea

If the scales show you have put on weight
If you've had a row with your best mate
If your period is two weeks late
Have a great big pot of tea

When you feel older than your age
When your budgie's pegged it in his cage
And you've three weeks left 'til your next wage
Have a great big pot of tea

Your twelve year old's had a tattoo
You've dropped your iPhone down the loo
And you've got more tash than Fu Manchu
You need a pot of tea

When there's water in your carburettor
And a massive hole in your French letter
You'll find that life feels so much better
With a great big pot of tea

When you've won a tenner on the nags
Your face pack's got rid of your bags
And that itching's just an itch – not crabs
Toast your luck with tea

When your new shoe's given you a blister
And your husband's run off with your sister
Or you've chucked up in game of Twister
Have a great big pot of tea

When you're standing in the slowest queue
And done a fart but followed through
Go home, get changed and have a brew
From a great big pot of tea

As Brits we cluster around the teapot when we need to celebrate or commiserate more than we do around a champagne bottle. This little poem celebrates our love affair with a pot of tea (Yorkshire tea obviously).

Paradox

Emerald Eyes
Midnight fur
Insistent mew
Rumbling purr
Silken whiskers
Velvet paws
Loving head butts
Lethal claws
Russian gymnast
Balance skill
Serial slayer
Thirst to kill
Fearless hunter
Meek and sweet
Sleek and fragile
Athlete
Independent

Attention greedy
Indifferent
Affection needy
Lazy sleeper
Hurtling blur
Fussy diner
Scavenger
What a paradox
you are
God in heaven's avatar
Or perhaps a demon's
Deft design
Dear familiar
of mine

What a paradox a cat is. They demand attention one minute, then scratch you when they get it. I have a weakness for black cats and have never been without one. They get unfair bad press, their image tied up with superstition. My black cats have been the most affectionate I've ever had. But on their terms, obviously.

Trust

Today
He broke her favourite vase
It lay on the bedroom floor
Shattered
A hundred shards and more

She glued it back together
Sure she had picked up all the pieces
That lay at her feet
She had taken time in mending it
So why was it incomplete?

It looked like the vase he bought her
But the cracks still showed
And it would no longer hold water

After taking back an unfaithful boyfriend, I tried very hard to make it work but the past couldn't be undone and I couldn't unknow that he'd shagged the local barmaid (barmaids plural as I later found out).

Don't

Don't pick me up and slobber
Over me as if I'm cake
Affection's mine to give
It's not for you to take

Don't assume I'll ever come
When you call out my name
Don't think that you can train me
Because I don't play that game

Don't plonk me on your knee
Presuming I'll want to be there
I will choose the when and why
The how and who and where

Don't ever trust my purr
Means I'm settled and I'm calm
I can switch it off like 'that'
And sink my teeth into your arm

Don't wish that I'll feel sorry
For bringing home a half-dead mouse
Don't be a screaming spoilsport
Let me chase it round the house

Don't hope that I will change
So save your censure and your wrath
I'm proud combo of a cutie
And a simmering psychopath

A poem about why cats will never conform to our 'pet' ideal. Why should they? We love them regardless. Plus they don't really give a toss what we think anyway.

The Elvis Presley Gift Shop

In the Elvis Presley gift shop
There are lots of Elvis Presley things
Elvis Presley pendants, tee shirts
Matches and plastic keyrings
There's Elvis pens and pencils
For all the budding writers
And Elvis Presley hip-swivelling oil
For sufferers of arthritis
For the kids there's paint by numbers
Colour him in it's all the rage
Buy canisters of Elvis sweat
And smell like him on stage

There's Elvis Presley condoms
To set all hearts aflutter
Cos they taste of quarter-pounders
Bacon, lard and peanut butter
Eyelashes, snippets of Elvis's toenails
And a genuine Elvis tooth
And a hundred more original molars
In the stockroom in the roof
There's some musical vibrators
A choice I see of two
One plays 'All Shook Up'
And the other 'Stuck on You.'
There's Elvis Presley quilts and sheets
And Elvis tasselled pillows
Big wigs, false tits and make up kits
For all would-be Priscillas
There are Elvis Presley teddy bears
And Elvis clotted cream fudge
And Elvis Presley laxatives
For when your bowels need a nudge

The girl behind the counter
Is the owner's latest flame
'Nice to meet you, boy,' she said
Telling me her name
Was Lisa Marie Graceland
Now, that I was surprised to learn
Cos her parents have a veg shop
On a street in Wath on Dearne
She wears an Elvis top: 'THE KING LIVES ON'
And a big black hairy quiff
Don't take the piss
She'll crush your jailhouse rocks
If you said he was just a stiff
Elvis lives on all right, the words ring out
On plates and cups and saucers
Emblazoned with pictures of him, fat and thin
On stage and in the forces
I am obliged to buy something
From this Elvis enterprise
Cos Lisa Marie is watching me
With serial killer eyes
I buy an Elvis CD
So I can hear him croon
Blue Christmas and Suspicious Minds
In pure pitch perfect tune
For though the man went downhill
And started wearing trousers
That would fit around a fat bloke
Plus a row of terraced houses

Went through women like a hound dog
Had some really dodgy parties
Trusted all the wrong folk
Popped pills like they were smarties
When he died at only forty-two
The world wept at the news
Cos there'd never be another
Who could fill his blue suede shoes

I was once in a souvenir shop in Greece that had the tackiest selection of goods I have ever seen in my life, including – for no reason I can think of other than they'd bought a job lot of rejects from a Graceland pound shop – lots of Elvis souvenirs. The King deserved so much better than to have his image on tat.

Work

A partridge in a big bull's field
Looked sad as sad can be
He sighed 'I wish that I were at
The top of that pear tree
But I'm too weak to fly that far'
The bull said 'Eat my droppings
They're packed with energising stuff
You'll fly like Mary Poppins'
The partridge was excited
'Cheers, mate, that's what I'll do'
So off he went across the field
To eat the big bull's pooh
He flew up to the highest branch
'Look at me' he said
But then the farmer raised his gun
And bang, the bird dropped... dead
There's a moral to this story
So listen and beware:
Bullshit can get you to the top
But it won't keep you there

A cautionary tale. Though, to be fair, I've worked in many a place where the 'partridges' have hung on in right up there. Sadly.

The School Reunion

You'll find that the class reunion
Is never arranged by the one
Who's a bankrupt, a drunk
A prat peddling skunk
Or the girl who's put on twenty ston'

Bev held the do at her mansion
She was loaded, a business high flyer
She looked totally fantastic
Though she was mostly plastic
And would melt if she stood near a fire

Sam used to be top lad in Science
But now he's gone all arty-farty
Fred was a fat chunk
But now he's a hunk
And runs his own school of karate

Ken was the rough kid whose mum was a scruff
Renowned for a wide range of smells
He came from a mess
But he's now a success
And owns a whole chain of hotels

Sharon talks posh and is glamorous
She works for a company in France
I was nearly in bits
Cos at school she had nits
And a habit of wetting her pants

Lynn was spotty and lanky
The school bitches made her life hell
But the ugly duckling has gone
And Lynn's now a swan
Who models for Coco Chanel

Mandy was always a bit thick at school
Especially rubbish at maths
I wasn't surprised
That her family comprised
Of eight kids to nine different dads

Simon's as big as his gob now
In the old days he was really skinny
He drives a large car
Top range Jaguar
Cos he can't fit his arse in a mini

Andrew turned up in a twin set and pearls
He said he weren't in a good place
Until he became Jilly
Got rid of his willy
Now he wears a broad smile on his face

Stu has a shop selling sarnies
Keith is a refuse collector
Tim's a contractor
And Jack is an actor
Who impersonates Hannibal Lecter

Philip flogs sweets on the market
Jim's a large animal vet
Jane caused a stir
She's an entrepreneur
Who sells her dirty knickers on't Net

Les had long locks like a rock star
All the girls could have ate him for dinner
He looked like Brian May
So assume our dismay
To find now he's the spit of Yul Brynner

Sal drives trains, Brian drives taxis
Tez is a singer on ships
Baz plays the drums
And Kaz staples tums
To stop lard-arses scoffing on chips

There were only three no shows I noticed
Sue lives in Australia now
I was totally delighted
That we weren't reunited
Cos I hated the horrible cow

Finley was always the 'boy who'd go far'
So it came to us all as a shock
To learn teacher's pet
Smuggled drugs to Phuket
And he's now in jail in Bangkok

And Alan, who was the class heart-throb
Tall, handsome and funny and flirty
So awfully unfair
That he caught something rare
Didn't even make it to thirty

We walked part of our journey together
It was lovely to see everyone
We were glad that we came
We all said the same
That our schooldays were lit up with fun

The playground's a long distant memory
As are PE and History and Sums
But we took from our meeting
How life can be fleeting
We should make each day count when it comes

Thanks to the rise of social media, in recent years old friends from way back have got in touch and it's been a joy to catch up and find out where they are and what they're doing. There are a couple of exceptions in every class though – those you hope never to bump into again. And sadly, tales of those who passed too young. Grab life whilst it's here and now, folks!

May Bluebells

If I could catch the scent of bluebells
And set it free to bring
The ghosts of long-dead aunts to me
And picnics in the spring
Would I uncork their fragrance
In the heat of August's blaze
To help me find the path again
To faded childhood days
Or as the wind whips autumn leaves
Or snowdrops gently fall
Should I compel the bluebells
To answer to my call?
For they belong in fairy woods
Legion wild and still
In untamed banks of silent blue
And May's damp earthy chill
And butterflies of memories
That visit with the scent
To flit beloved 'cross the heart
Like them, for May, were meant

No one waits for anything any more. We all want everything now on demand. But sometimes things are sweeter for the wait. Sometimes it's good to enjoy May and bluebells and the memories they evoke in their rightful time because then they retain their specialness. Nature should call the shots where bluebells are concerned.

Siblings

Remember how we used to fight
When we were only small
I'd push you down the staircase
You'd slam me 'gainst a wall
And when we shared the bath water
You'd always do a wee
So I'd roll some massive bogeys
And flick them in your tea
You'd call me lots of horrid names
Like Fatty, Smelly, Swot
And I'd punch your living daylights out
Every chance I got
We'd batter one another
With any apparatus
And mum would come in shouting
As she tried to separate us
'One day you two will be great friends
Just you wait and see'
And now I say with hand on heart
...How wrong can someone be?

I don't have siblings so I had two children in quick succession so they'd have a playmate. However, they were constantly fighting when they were little and the man who ran the nursery 'Uncle Derek' told me that he and his brother were just the same. 'But you're good mates now?' I said, presuming. Uncle Derek replied, 'No, we never did get on.'

Karma is a Bitch

It's a bit rich
To say that
Karma is a bitch
She's a pal, your best mate
The one that says
'Don't cry, just wait
Let me finish this drink
This cigarette
I'll be there soon
I won't forget
Chin up, stay strong
Get on with things
And leave me
Lurking in the wings
Be calm
Controlled
I am the dish
That's best served cold
The poison
With no antidote
The chicken bone
Lodged in the throat

The itch
They cannot find to scratch
Eggs of envy
Warmed to hatch
The sweet success
That skirts their trap
To land
Into another's lap
Considerably more fun
And witty
To pull the rug
When they're sitting pretty
My mill grinds slow
It takes its time
But trust me, darling
It grinds fine
No one escapes
My ancient law
After all
What are friends for?'

Maybe she is a bitch
But (fingers crossed)
She's my bitch

Just a playful little piece. I do rather like the idea that Karma is a friend who takes on the burden of exacting revenge and telling you that it might happen later rather than sooner… but rest assured, it will happen. Oh I wish.

Mills & Boon

I once picked up a Mills & Boon
I thought it would be shit
But I read the first two pages
And fell head first into it

The heroine was a perfect peach
The hero stinking rich
Then there was a love decoy
Who was a nasty bitch

The heroine hated him on sight
She saw herself as prey
And though he swore that she'd be his
She fought him all the way

He was arrogant and bossy
Not a man you'd want to kiss
Like the heroine I thought
'Who does that wanker think he is?'

As the story flowed
We found the hero wasn't arsey
He was Rochester incarnate
Or a sexy Mr Darcy

But as our heroine realised
He was a man to trust
Along comes floozy pouting
Flashing baby blues and bust

Our hero's eyes have turned to her
I was filled with abject rage
'Don't go there lad, she's awful'
I shouted madly at the page

But t'was a sly red herring
Our hero wasn't fickle
There was just one girl he wanted
For a bit of slap and tickle

But only when they'd wed of course
Our hero was a gent
The floozy was kicked to the kerb
And I was left content

I read another and another
Each different, yet the same
The plots wound round the houses
Then that perfect ending came

The hero was a sheik, a doc
French, Greek sometimes Italian
A playboy, multi-millionaire
But every time a stallion

The heroine always innocent
Whilst being ripe for bedding
The floozy always vile
And you'd love to kick her head in

It really didn't matter
That conclusions were foregone
For the thrill was in the journey
That the author took me on

I can't begin to tell you
What joy my heart amassed
Whilst reading Mills & Boons
From first page right through to last

For when life had dealt me lemons
When romance was on a ration
Those books kept all my hopes afloat
Of finding love and passion

In the early 80s we took my Nan to Malta with the family and none of our suitcases arrived for days except one of hers which was full only of Mills & Boon books from the library. Starved of reading material I had no alternative but to read one of these and I fell in love with them to the extent that they had a massive influence on how I was to write - ie a predictably happy ending guaranteed for the reader so they could sit back and enjoy the journey knowing they were in the author's safe hands.

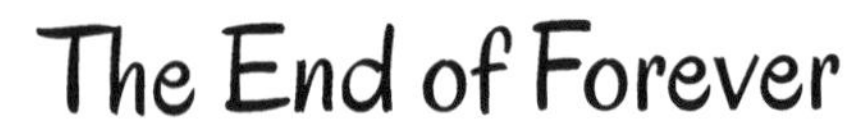

The End of Forever

You both start off as soul mates
As the very best of friends
Lovers for forever
...And then forever ends

The signs were there I know
That we had sailed too far off course
There was no turning back
The sole solution: a divorce

His photo was stuck on the wall
For me to throw my darts in
My pubes grew like a forest
I no longer kept my farts in

When he came home, there was no kiss
No dotingly made tea
When I bought dine in meals for two
Both portions were for me

I threw out all my stockings
I wore peep-hole bras no more
My knickers reached up to my neck
My nightie down t' floor

I used his razor in the bath
Though I knew it blunt the blades
He stopped closing the bog door
When he dropped his stink grenades

My life was fifty shades of beige
Dull as a play by Ibsen
My fantasies were full
Of shouting 'Freedom' like Mel Gibson

I no longer shaved my tash off
I no longer watched my figure
Well I did, I filled it full of cake
And watched it growing bigger

And during the rare bonks
I no longer screamed for more
I couldn't bear to stay awake
I'd just lie there and snore

The only thing that made me smile
While living in that farce
Was to use the cloth he saved just for his face
To wash my arse

Where once we used to talk, to laugh
There barely was a grunt
And in the place of 'darling' 'babe'
Were names that rhymed with 'stunt'

Our home became a war zone
Worse than bombed and blitzed Beirut
As we rumbled to the finish line
And our decree absolute

The love between us warped too far
For chance of realignment
I felt trapped, imprisoned, lonely
Like a solitary confinement

Yet there was a time he looked at me
As if I was Nigella
And I could not imagine life
With any other fella

Once we were forever but
We broke and couldn't be mended
And the best day of our marriage
Was the day forever ended

I was married after a whirlwind romance – more wind than whirl it has to be said. My divorce cost me a fortune. It was, however, the best money I ever spent. But I often wondered how that initial high peak of heady love had inverted to form that low spike of abhorrence. Where does all that affection go?

The Sleepy Cat

I think I'll have a little sleep
I think I'll have a snore
I think I'll wake up for a wee
And then I'll sleep some more

I think I'll have my dinner
Then I'll climb upon your lap
So you can stroke my fur
Whilst I take a little nap

I think I'll try a wander
Have a little knock about
Catch a bird and then come home
For that will surely tire me out

I think I'll open up one eye
And take a sneaky peep
The moon is in the sky – or sun
...That means it's time to sleep

Cats sleep on average 15 hours per day. Mine couldn't sleep more if they were stuffed.

Princesses

We would have got on like a house on fire
Princess Di and me
We'd have bonded over lots of carbs
And great big pots of tea
In her Prada and my Primark
We'd have moaned about our weight
And done some serious bitchin'
'Bout those women that we hate
We'd have fessed up all our stresses
And shared our dreams and hopes
And found that we both hole up
To watch soppy films and soaps
We'd have talked about our lads
And all sorts of mother things
Like trying to keep them safe
As they start to stretch their wings
We'd have laughed about our exes
What a useless bunch of farts
And cried about the hungry
Prince-shaped hole
Within our hearts

One thing I have learned over the years is that women's friendship knocks down barriers of creed and colour, age and background. Princess Diana, despite all her privileges, was just a girl like most of us who wanted a heart full of contentment. I think, if we'd met, we would have had more similarities than differences, give or take the tiaras (mine is from Claire's Accessories).

Christmas Carols Everywhere

Carols in the bandstand
Carols in Birdwell
Carols outside Greggs
KFC and Taco Bell
Carols up in Cawthorne
Carols in the pub
Carols in the Town Hall
And in Jump Working Mens Club
Carols loud and jolly
Carols in the snow
On the back seat of the bus
And underneath the mistletoe
Carols in the market
Carols round the tree
...That Carol puts herself about
Almost as much as me

For many years I was a writer of greetings card copy and this was one of the poems I wrote to sit on a Christmas card, which sold particularly well. I love to perform this – it always gets a laugh (after a few Proseccos imbibed by my audience). I used local village names – yes there really is a place called Jump near Barnsley. The bus to it was called the 'Jump Circular' and every time we saw it, we used to jump around in a circle. As kids obviously – not adults. Well, not sober adults anyway.

A Woman's Perfect Christmas

No work for simply ages
No relatives in sight
A fridge stocked up with goodies
With nothing labelled 'lite'
A fire crackling in the grate
A scented Christmas tree
Sole use of the remote control
For a ninety-inch TV
Champagne by the bucketful
But only premier cru
And stacks of gorgeous presents
From De Beers and Jimmy Choo
A perfectly cooked dinner
Delivered to my door
And a little bell to ring
Should I require any more
Snowflakes at the window
Mistletoe on the ceiling
And under it with puckered lips
A hunk who's most appealing
He's generous with his stuffing
And passionate love we'll make
And when it gets to ten o'clock
He'll turn into a cake

Too often we end up pleasing other people at Christmas more than ourselves. But if we could have just one selfish Christmas… this is what I'd have.

The Omniscient Santa

He knows when you've been naughty
He knows when you've been nice
He knows your every virtue
And he knows your every vice
He knows when you've been sleeping
He knows when you're awake
He knows when you've been dieting
And when you've been scoffing cake
He knows when you've been happy
He knows when you've been blue
He knows when you've been skiving
Telling work you've got the flu
He knows when you've been sober
He knows when you've been plastered
He knows when you've been good or bad
Cos he's a nosy bastard

The older I've got, the more I've been disturbed about the idea of a strange old man going into children's bedrooms with the full blessing of their parents. Especially to empty his sacks. Operation Yewtree anyone?

The Mystery Man

Who is that mystery man
Who creeps into your house
Just as the clock strikes midnight
He's as quiet as a mouse
He doesn't come in through the door
You do not know he's there
You cannot hear his boots
As they step softly up the stair
Who is that mystery man
With a massive, bulging sack
Full of lots of goodies
That he carries on his back
Who is that mystery man
Who leaves so silently?

...He's a bloody sodding burglar
And he's nicked your new TV

A Christmas poem with no explanation needed. Keep your doors, windows and chimneys locked at all times.

The Snowman

I made myself a snowman
As handsome as could be
I sculpted him like Johnny Depp
So he could sleep with me
I moulded him strong shoulders
I gave him bulging pecs
And a look upon his face
That said 'My darling, let's have sex'
At last, I thought, a man
Who will be faithful to the end
He won't get pissed and show me up
Or flirt with my best friend
I cuddled up beside him
Drifted off to sweet repose
I woke to find he'd buggered off
Left just his carrot nose
I was gutted that he turned out
Not to be that great a catch
For no gentleman would ever
Make me sleep in his wet patch

Even men you make can't always be relied on to hang around.

T'was Neet Afore Christmas

T'was neet afore Christmas when all through the house
Not a creature was stirring, not even a mouse
The whippets were snoring all snug in their beds
While visions of dried pigs' ears danced in their heads
And I in my curlers with Baileys nightcap
Had just settled down for a long winter's nap
When out on the lawn there arose such a clatter
I sprang from my pit to see what was the matter
Oh God not some hoodie with drug-addled brain
Out to kill me for pence just to buy crack cocaine
But no, t'was a sleigh landing lively and quick
I knew in a moment it must be St Nick
He was leading eight reindeer all cuddly and tame

And he whistled and shouted and called them by name
'Now Gemma, now Stella, now Gaga and Whitney
On Cheryl, On Shannon, On Rylan and Britney'
(Alas even in these traditional rhymes
Names are obliged to move with the times)
His eyes how they twinkled, his nose like a cherry
He made straight for my bottle of Bristol Cream sherry
He eyed the mince pie in the hearth with remorse
That it wasn't from Greggs and was pork with brown sauce
He was weighty with chins, a right jolly elf
Beard excepted, he looked quite a lot like myself
Though red's not forgiving and had I been him
I'd have gone for all black with a fake sable trim

His sack was a-heaving with iPhones and iPods
'Eeh the kids of today' he said 'Spoilt little sods
They don't want some nuts in small hanging socks
They want five hundred quid and a bloody Xbox'
He laughed like a drain then 'Long as they're right
You can't have bairns sad cos their presents are shite'
Then spotting the carrots he said 'Oh that's kind
To have the concerns of my reindeer in mind
They so love their carrots they'll have quite a feast
And then won't stop farting 'til Easter at least'
He looked at his list 'Now let me see
What, little lady, did you ask from me?'
'A Tiffany bracelet' I said 'three Mont Blanc pens,
George Clooney in pants and a Mercedes Benz'
I tried, but it came as little surprise
To get Thorntons and books and some slippers my size
He burped up some pie like a typical bloke
Then adjusted his crotch and fastened his cloak
He gave me a wink and bid me adieu
Then called to his reindeer and sprang up my flue
They rose to the sky and there in formation
Flew faster away than Jimmy Savile's reputation
But I heard Santa shout as he guided his fleet
'Happy Christmas, dear Yorkshire
God bless and good neet'

I wrote this for a bit of fun to perform – my take on 'A Visit from St Nicholas'. It's written in Yorkshire dialect as we all know Santa came from here - whatever anyone else tells you. Incidentally the same place that God comes from.

The Language of God

There's them that mash potatoes
But in Yorkshire we mash tea
Elite is something we put on
So we can flipping see

A spell is not what witches cast
It's a tiny piece of wood
And Roger Moore's what men can do
With Viagra in their blood

Mooing's nowt to do with cows
It sits in t'sky at neet
And tours aren't trips on buses
They're the ends of people's feet

Food causes complications
We differ from the bourgeoisie
For their lunchtime is our dinner
And their dinnertime our tea

And then we come to teacakes
Another point that's moot
Because here they are just breadcakes
Without a hint of fruit

Add currants to the bread mix
Bake – and then you'll see
That you'll have *currant teacakes*
How much simpler can it be

Darn's nowt to do with sewing
It's the opposite to up
And Yorkshire Tea's the only tea
That we will ever sup

Quoits to us are things with sleeves
Not a sort of hoopla game
We put coils inside our oils (!)
But I think they do the same

Brexit is a phrase
We're sick of seeing everywhere
Here it's what a fat lass does
To a flimsy plastic chair

Black bright means that it's mucky
And salad's a 'cold snap'
And south is anywhere below
Doncaster on the map

And Tin Tin's not a cartoon
It's a Yorkshirewoman's wail
When she's in bed with a mister
Who's got a tiny tail

I could wax lyrical for ages
About our words unique
But suffice to say our language
Is what God himself would speak

I could have made this poem a million verses long with all the unique words and phrases that we use in Yorkshire or, as we call it, 'God's Own County'. I collect them and just when I think I've found them all, up another one pops. I've printed most of them on a tea towel which is – ahem – available from my website. They've been posted all over the world and are hanging in homes and bars from Sydney to Scarborough, Plymouth to Papua New Guinea.

Instead

You could have said, I looked pretty in red
Instead
of you look crap in blue
you could have said
my new hairdo
was phwoar
Instead
of well it's less of an eyesore
than it was before
you could have said
I had a Kardashian arse
Instead
of you look inbred, you look wank
a big fat slapper
the bastard child of a Sherman tank
and an obese Barbapapa
you could have told the doc
you were suffering from tension
Instead
you said the missus was so fucking ugly
you needed Viagra intervention
you could have filled my heart with love

Instead
you stuffed it full of dread
you could have fled
made someone else your wife
given me the chance to lead a peaceful life
left me with a shred
of myself
to grow, live unafraid
Instead
you stayed
in my bed
left nothing cruel unsaid
savoured how my ego bled

And so I killed you
...and now you're dead

One of my deeper poems, albeit with a twist. 'Mrs Instead' got off with a sympathetic sentence and went on to live a very happy life, in case you're asking.

A Yorkshire Valentine

Tha nivver buys me chocolates
Tha's nivver fetched me flowers
And when tha's been in toilet
The pong hangs round for hours
Tha must have been born in a barn
Cos tha nivver shuts a door
And when tha comes in from artside
Tha trails mud all oeert floor
The closest that tha's ever got
To romantic oratory
Is to say 'Eeeh lass, tha not all bad
Tha'll do alreight for me'
Tha keeps me wekken snooring
Tha teks up all the bed
And tha's doubled up in size
Since the day that we were wed
And when tha teks thi booits off
Tha can't imagine t'smell
But would I change thi for the world?
No – would I bloody hell

A friend of mine could never stand flowers because her husband used to buy them for her after he'd been caught out with another woman. He'd roll out all the empty gestures as he pleaded for another chance: jewellery, champagne, soppy cards, huge bouquets. She's now with a no-nonsense and very kind Yorkshireman who treats her like a queen so she can put up with the fact that he's a messy bugger.

Internet Dating

I went on an internet dating site
To hook up with my heart's desire
But all I found on it were losers
Every man there a fake or a liar

Sam described himself as cuddly
When in fact he was morbidly obese
His arse was the size of Slovenia
And his nipples sat snug on his knees

Fred said he was Hugh Jackman's double
I thought 'Oh my lord I am in luck'
In the flesh he looked like Quasimodo
After he'd been run o'er by a truck

Drake was as tight as a duck's arse
His mean streak was just a bit much
Now don't get me wrong on a first date
I always expect to go Dutch

But he took me for 'afternoon tea'
To a place where they served a cheap brew
He bought an egg butty to share and – the nerve!
He split my French fancy in two

'I come from a close family' said Timbo
Who was hoping to be my new lover
Then I found out his gran was also his aunt
And his uncle was also his brother

Alexander smelt of desperation
It was clear he was after a screw
If a girl had a pulse he'd be in there
And I think if she didn't, she'd still do

In contrast Ken was extra fussy
His date should not drink smoke or swear
No fatties no gingers, no thickies no mingers
No make-up and no pubic hair

You'd have thought with a list long as that lot
That Ken would be some sort of god
He was squat with a paunch and all warty
With a face like a disgruntled cod

'I like to do all things by candlelight'
Said Romantic Leeds Gentleman Will
He had no choice but to use lots of candles
He'd not paid his utility bill

Martin said that he was at least six foot three
He was fourteen inch shorter in stature
And the photo he sent was so dated
He was posing with Margaret Thatcher

Trev was tall, handsome and gorgeous
I thought he was like an Adonis
But when he said he liked to gamble
He meant he wouldn't wear rubber johnnies

Mike was a master at massage
My spirits rose high and then sank
When I found him fiddling with my iPad
Trying to massage the brass from my bank

Anthony wrote that clothes were constraints
And he couldn't wait to get to know me
He bragged he was built like a racehorse
And then sent me a dick-pic to show me

My first date with Frank – a disaster!
I thought this is no casual fling
When I was halfway through my Nandos
And he pulled out a solitaire ring

He said 'I'm lonely there's no point in waiting
Come share my house and my life
Just leave moving in 'til after next week
Cos that's when I'm burying my wife'

Vin was in touch with his feminine side
He was lovely, I thought 'this one will do'
But he arrived stinking heavily of Rive Gauche
And dressed up like Danny La Rue

'I think barriers are things to be flattened'
Said Open-Minded from Doncaster Daniel
And would I fancy an orgy with his ex Marie
Her neighbours and their Cocker Spaniel

Don said he was a top sportsman
What he meant was he liked watching darts
Brian had been on Britain's Got Talent
He performed Nessun Dorma with farts

Phil said he liked to try new things out
I was intrigued until I came to find
He meant greasing some objects with trifle
And inserting them in my behind

I was fed up and jaded I tell you
Then I got a nice message from Finn
A man so refreshingly honest
Does just what it says on the tin

My internet dating is over
We married and everything's bright
It just goes to prove it can work out
Cos there's diamonds in there with the shite

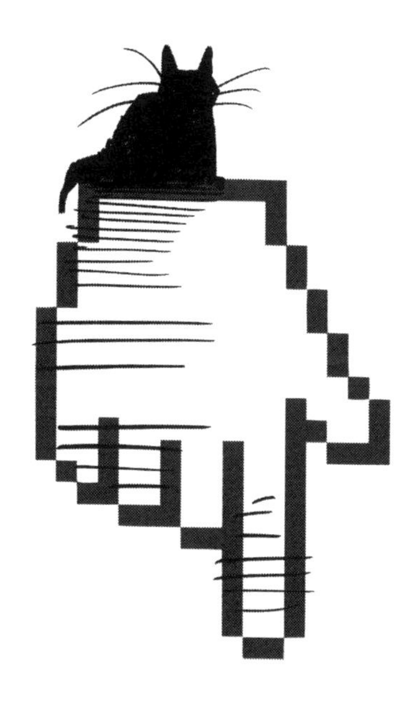

I did have a stab at internet dating. I met some lovely men and some quite scary ones and a policeman who was determined to get all my savings out of me so he could spend them on his ancient secret girlfriend (if ever there was a book plot!). Lots of my friends met wonderful partners online and are joyously happy, so it can work if you're wise and careful.

The Sayings of Mum

If the wind changes you'll stay like that
Don't make me come o'er there
Eat all your crusts they're good for you
They'll give you curly hair

Am I talking to a brick wall?
Money does not grow on trees
There are kids starving in Africa
Who'd be grateful for those peas

I don't care who started it
Your room is a pigsty
This is a home not a hotel
Because I said so, that's why

Eating sugar causes worms
If you get them you'll be sorry
Always wear clean pants
In case you're knocked down by a lorry

You don't know how lucky you are
You live these days like kings
Call me when you get there
Or at least give me three rings

You're going nowhere dressed like that
Were you born in a barn?
Those ears could grow potatoes
You'll put me in the funny farm

What did your last slave die of?
This hurts me more than you
If Darren Jones jumped off a cliff
Would you jump off it too?

Will you please put a sock in it
I can't hear myself think
Just wait until your dad gets home
...No wonder why I drink!

I never thought I'd spout all the many sayings my mother spouted at me and no doubt her mother spouted at her. But we do. We all do...

Carpe Diem

Don't let your final words be
Wish I'd acted in a play
Wish I'd gone for ballet lessons
Wish I'd flown a bird of prey

Wish I'd done a course in Spanish
Wish I'd learned to play guitar
Gone to the Ritz in London
Just to order caviar

Wish I'd learned to dance a tango
Wish I'd waved that job goodbye
Wish I'd dyed my hair bright purple
When I still had hair to dye

Wish I'd Eurostarred to Paris
Wish I weren't full of regret
That I never flew to Vegas
Bet a grand on the roulette

Wish I'd thrown a lump of clay
Upon a potter's wheel
Wish I'd rung a big church bell
Wish I'd tried a jellied eel

Wish I'd booked that bloody cruise
Wish I'd bought myself that Jag
Or the Christian Louboutins
With a tart-red matching bag

Wish I'd left my other half
The evil nasty twat
And moved into a cottage
With a budgie and a cat

Wish I'd gone to see my favourite group
Before they all retired
Wish I'd met up with old friends
Before they all expired

Washed my bottom in a bidet
Toured the Hermitage Museum
Wish I'd grabbed life by the balls
Learned the art of *carpe diem*

Why did I never climb K2
Or snorkel in the sea?
Why did I never write that book
That's sitting inside me?

Don't let fear stand in your way
Don't let self-doubts hurt you
Don't think that you're not worth it
Don't let your derring-do desert you

However big, however small
A dream is still a dream
Live it before the curtain falls
And life runs out of steam

A dream's born to be realised
Not to rest upon a shrine
It's a fruit grown to be savoured
Not to wither on the vine

Don't be the one who wishes
That they'd played as hard as grafted
And opened up that shop
To sell the jewellery that they'd crafted

Or took that trip to Venice
Or sunbathed nude in Trinidad
Be the one that says 'Guess what
I chuffing did it – and I'm glad'

I'm always so grateful to whatever it was that pushed me to become an author because I would have dreaded to have reached eighty and not given my biggest dream my best shot. And I made it come true! If you have a dream in your heart – just go for it, is what I'm trying to say in this one. Dreams are born to be lived out, not sit inside you rotting. However big or small yours is – SEIZE THE DAY (which is the translation of the Latin title).

Who's the Boss?

'Who's the boss in this relationship?'
I asked the bloody cat
'I poop, you clear it up,' he said
'I think that answers that'

And to finish – a small poem about a cat. Anyone who has a cat will see where I'm coming from here. It is a common misconception that anyone owns a cat – the cat owns you. And don't you ever forget it.

The End
(of this poetic tail)

Thank you SO much for buying and supporting
Yorkshire Cat Rescue.

Biographies

Don't forget the old guys. Here's recently adopted Siamese Oscar, 15 with bad eyesight who is a total joy!

Milly Johnson is a Sunday Times bestselling author of fiction novels. She is also a professional joke-writer, scriptwriter, poet, newspaper columnist, after-dinner speaker, Vice President of the Yorkshire Society and patron of Yorkshire Cat Rescue. She was born, bred and resides in Yorkshire.

Find out more at
www.millyjohnson.co.uk
Instagram: @themillyjohnson
Facebook: millyjohnsonauthor
Twitter: @millyjohnson

Stuart Gibbins has worked in the design industry for over 40 years. Clients include Milly Johnson and Lynda La Plante along with lots of people who aren't famous.

His work can be found at stuartgibbins.com and nm4s.com.

Printed in Great Britain
by Amazon